# Electoral College What?

Dana Fernandez

Illustrated by Kiera Pagano

*Electoral College What?*

*Copyright © 2020 Dana Fernandez.*

*This is a work of fiction. All of the characters, names, incidents, organizations, and dialogue in this novel are either the products of the author's imagination or are used fictitiously.*

*iUniverse books may be ordered through booksellers or by contacting:*

*iUniverse*
*1663 Liberty Drive*
*Bloomington, IN 47403*
*www.iuniverse.com*
*844-349-9409*

*ISBN: 978-1-6632-0788-3 (sc)*
*ISBN: 978-1-6632-0790-6 (hc)*
*ISBN: 978-1-6632-0789-0 (e)*

*Library of Congress Control Number: 2020916327*

*Print information available on the last page.*

*iUniverse rev. date: 09/25/2020*

Dedicated to my amazing son Luca, my inspiration.

"Welcome to Social Studies class!" Mrs. Robinson proudly greets her new students waiting to enter the classroom. Longtime friends Luca and George stand next to each other in the hallway just outside the classroom. Luca turns to George and, in a most excited voice, says, "Oh, I can't wait!" Luca has always had a fondness for learning history.

George, on the other hand … His expression says it all as he looks at Luca in the most pathetic way to say, "Oh, I'm going to hate this."

There is nothing Mrs. Robinson enjoys more than teaching her students something new and challenging. Since the November presidential election is fast approaching, this, Mrs. Robinson thinks to herself, is the perfect time to introduce the students to the real voting process in the United States.

"I'm so excited, class, and you will be too! Today, we are going to learn about something called the electoral college. So, let us begin!" Mrs. Robinson exclaims.

Luca's parents had been telling him there would be an election coming up soon. All he really knows about it is that his parents go to a voting center and cast their votes for the candidates they like. Not much to it, Luca thinks in his head, but he is most eager to hear what Mrs. Robinson has to say.

Luca turns to George and says, "Have you ever heard of the electoral college?"

George looks at Luca, sighs heavily, and mumbles as he puts his head down on the desk. "Yup, I'm really going to hate this."

Mrs. Robinson starts with a little history. She tells the class that in this country, we have a president who is elected every four years with a maximum of two terms, or a total of eight years, in office.

"The president of the United States is part of the executive branch of government. It's the executive branch's job to ensure that laws are followed."

She explains to the students that it is the people who vote, and that is called a democracy. "However, class, we have a special kind of democracy; it's a representative democracy or a republic."

Maddy, super excited, wants to share her thoughts by quickly chiming in with her hand flailing in the air, "We actually modeled our form of government after that of the ancient Romans. It was the Romans who …"

Mrs. Robinson interrupts. "Exactly, Maddy! Love the enthusiasm," she says with a smile. "In other words, we have elected representatives, or people in government who speak for the public. The United States of America has too large of a population for every single person to be able to go and vote on everything. These representatives serve in Congress, which is part of the legislative branch of government. Congress is made up of both the Senate and the House of Representatives. It is their job to make the laws. Finally, we have the judicial branch of government, which is made up of the justices of the Supreme Court. It is their job to interpret the laws. The Supreme Court can play an important role if the results in an election are ever in dispute.

"The main reason we even have three branches of government is so we have something called …"

"Ooh, ooh, ooh." Luca waves his hand high above his head.

"Yes, Luca?" Mrs. Robinson stops to say.

"Checks and balances!" Luca states as a matter of fact.

"Why, yes, Luca. Each branch keeps an eye on the other two so no one branch can ever become too powerful. Our Founding Fathers set up our government this way."

Mrs. Robinson is reviewing some basics in government to refresh the students' minds, but Luca is desperately waiting to hear about how the electoral college ties into all this. He already knows a lot about the US government.

"So far, so good, George?" Luca turns to George, who has already slouched so far down in his chair that the top of his head can barely be seen. George simply gives Luca a thumbs-up to show he is still there.

Then Mrs. Robinson gets to the part Luca is eagerly awaiting. "Similarly, in Article II of the Constitution, our Founding Fathers included something called the electoral college to be part of our election process. Think of the people in the electoral college almost like representatives from each state. Each state has its own process by which it assigns electors, although the number of electors is based on the population of the state. So not all states have the same number of electors."

"Mrs. Robinson, will we have our sixth grade election done this way too?" Maddy asks inquisitively.

"What a marvelous idea! We shall!" Mrs. Robinson says emphatically.

The president of the sixth grade had always been elected by popular vote. Luca is already starting to picture in his head what an election with electorates would look like.

"Now, the president is not voted into office by direct vote from the people but instead is voted into office by the electors from each state. Usually the candidate who wins the most votes in the state will take all the electoral votes in that state. This is true for all states except Maine and Nebraska, where sometimes the electors split their vote. To be president of the United States, you must reach two hundred seventy electoral votes from all the states combined. In the case of our sixth grade president, we will also be using the electoral votes to decide the winner."

Luca is hanging on to Mrs. Robinson's every word, except for the few times he nudges George to make sure he is still awake. Luca smiles as all the bits of information are pieced together in his mind. He understands how the electoral college makes a difference, and he grasps the importance of what Mrs. Robinson is teaching. Luca is happiest when he has learned something new that he can share with others.

As soon as class lets out, both boys head to lunch, where they quickly scarf down their food so they can go out to the playground. Luca is still reeling from all the information he got out of the lesson.

"Wow, did you know all that?" Luca practically jumps on George to ask the question.

"No. No … I still don't know all that," George responds with hesitation.

George cannot be happier to be out of that boring class and onto the playground, although the look on George's face rarely shows any kind of excitement as he almost always wears a permanent frown. It is just his way.

Luca continues, "So, do you get it, George?"

"Do I have to get it, Luca?" George replies.

"Yes. Yes you do! And yes you should! And yes you will, George!" Luca replies.

"Oh, man." George knows his friend, and he certainly knows that when Luca gets excited about something, he can talk about it for hours! There is really no point in fighting it, so George has learned to indulge Luca's interests.

"This is it, George. Voting begins here. This is where my parents go to cast their vote for their favorite candidate," Luca says.

"I got that, Luca. Adults go vote, then the votes get counted, and the candidate with the most votes becomes our next president," George says, proud of himself for having paid at least a little attention in class.

"Well, not quite," Luca goes on.

"You see, when you just count everyone's vote and the majority wins, that's called a popular vote. It is what would happen in a pure democracy, but we're not that. That was Athens during ancient times! We have a republic, and in a republic we have representation. Remember that Mrs. Robinson taught us about Congress and how we have the Senate where each state has two senators, and a House of Representatives, where each state has a number of representatives based on their population?"

George looks up as he is thinking. "Yeah, I remember that ... I think."

"Well, the electoral college is a group of people who are chosen by each political party. Usually we just think of the Democratic and the Republican Parties since they are the two major ones here in the United States. Each state's electorates are made up of how many representatives and senators they have in Congress. So, a big state like Texas, which has two senators and thirty-six representatives in Congress, would get thirty-eight electorates."

"Oh, okay," George says. "So, what exactly do these elected people do again?"

13

"Let's go back to the ballot box. When your parents check off which candidate they want to vote for, you might think they are voting for that candidate, but they are not! They are casting their vote for the electorates who represent that candidate. When the voting on Election Day in November is over, it is the electorates who have been chosen. Then in a separate vote in December is when the electoral college—that's all the electorates—go and cast their votes. They usually vote for the candidate who won the majority in their state," Luca explains to George.

"It sounds like double the work. I mean, the people already voted for the candidate they want, so why not just count all the votes?" George's interest seems to have been piqued a little, and now he really wants to understand why we have this process.

"Great question!" Luca exclaims.

"Picture it, George." Luca has his arm around George as he makes him envision. "Think classrooms, George—lots of sixth grade classes."

George, confused, asks, "What on earth do classrooms have to do with that elect … thing?"

"Let's have a mock election, and you'll see!" Luca declares with a devious grin. "Maddy and Jacob both want to be the sixth grade president, right? Well, first they would debate with each other like real candidates do. This is where they get a chance to tell all the students what they would do for them if they won. Then comes the vote. So, let's pretend Maddy and Jacob already had their election."

"Let's say this is how each classroom votes. Every student in each class has cast one vote for the candidate they want, either Maddy or Jacob. If we look at the totals from each class, then we see that Maddy has a total of fifty-three votes and Jacob has a total of sixty-seven votes. Who wins, George?" Luca asks.

"Jacob?" George intones his answer as a question.

"Well, yes and no, George. Remember that popular vote we talked about earlier? Jacob certainly won the popular vote because he simply got more individual votes. But remember the electoral college? Let's assign or give each classroom electorates based on their population, similar to how states have. Then, if all the electorate votes from one class go to the candidate who won that class, the result would be different. Maddy has a total of fourteen electoral votes, and Jacob has a total of eleven electoral votes, so Maddy wins." Luca finishes his point feeling accomplished.

"How is that fair?" George asks. "Shouldn't the person with the most votes win? Why even bother having the electoral college votes? I still don't get that." George shrugs his shoulders.

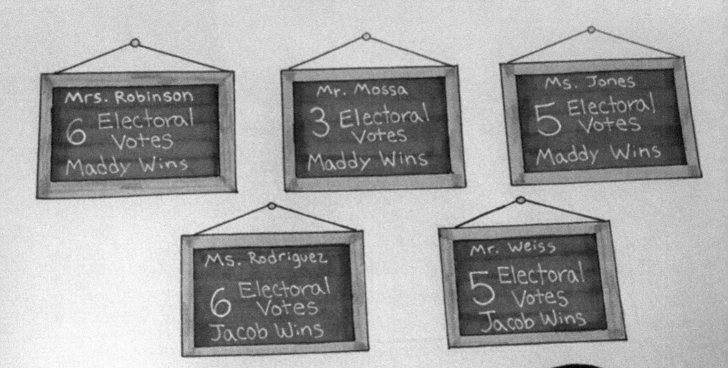

Maddy is the new Class President!

"Way back when, George, during the time of our Founding Fathers, it was decided that a purely democratic process wasn't going to work, as it hadn't in the past. It was not just about having the majority rule; it was about good government. Many people are uninformed and just vote for someone because their friend voted for that person," Luca explains.

"I've done that!" George chimes in.

"Exactly, George." Luca laughs.

"Some of our Founding Fathers wanted Congress to elect our president. A lot of people disagreed with that because then the people would not have a say. So, there was a compromise. That compromise is the electoral college. It's actually written into our Constitution, which you know is the highest law in the land!" Luca says.

"Yes. Mrs. Robinson talks about the importance of our Constitution all the time, Luca. It's in Article II. It's not like I never paid attention. Sheesh." George rolls his eyes.

Luca continues, "The electoral college makes sure that each state is fairly represented, whether it is a big state like California or a small state like Rhode Island. Sometimes it's easy to cheat to get more votes, but if you don't know which electoral votes will make a difference for the win, then it's a lot harder to cheat. It also does not matter whether you win a state by a lot of votes or just a few votes, because you usually end up with all the state's electoral votes."

"All the state's electoral votes go to the candidate who wins the state, except in Maine and Nebraska!" George declares proudly.

"By George, I think he's got it!" Luca says, laughing.

"This way, each candidate has to pay attention to all the states in order to win, not just the most populated ones. Our Founding Fathers really knew what they were doing."

Luca turns to George and asks, "What do you think, George?"

"I think I'm glad I'm not old enough to vote yet." Luca and George both laugh as they head off back to class.

**ballot box.** A secure place where people place their votes.

**candidate.** A person running for an elected government position.

**checks and balances.** Rules so no one branch of government becomes too powerful.

**Congress.** Part of the legislative branch of government that has two houses—the House of Representatives and the Senate.

**Constitution.** A written set of laws that govern a country, state, or other political organization.

**debate.** A discussion between two or more people where different opinions are expressed.

**democracy.** A form of government where people have a say in how the government is run by voting.

**Democratic Party.** One of the two major political parties in the United States in which people tend to be more "liberal" or "progressive."

**election.** The process of voting for a candidate.

**electoral college.** A group of electors from each state that forms every four years to elect the president of the United States.

**electors.** People elected or appointed to be part of the electoral college.

**executive branch.** The branch of government that includes the president; it is in charge of protecting the people and ensuring laws are followed.

**judicial branch.** The branch of government that includes the Supreme Court; it is in charge of interpreting the laws.

**legislative branch.** The branch of government that includes Congress; it is in charge of making laws.

**mock.** Not real; pretend.

**political party.** A group of people organized by their shared beliefs and goals. Two main political parties are the Democrats and the Republicans.

**popular vote.** General public vote.

**pure democracy.** A form of government used by the ancient Athenians where every citizen had to vote.

**representatives.** People elected or appointed to act or speak for other people.

**republic.** A form of government where people elect or appoint representatives to act or speak for them in government.

**Republican Party.** One of the two major political parties in the United States where people tend to be more "conservative."

**senators.** People elected to the Senate. There are two senators elected from each state.

**Supreme Court.** The highest court in the United States. There are nine Supreme Court justices (judges).

**US Constitution.** The highest law in the United States.

CPSIA information can be obtained
at www.ICGtesting.com
Printed in the USA
BVHW050746231020
591519BV00003B/32